Usborne First Experiences

The New Puppy

Anne Civardi

Illustrated by Stephen Cartwright

Edited by Michelle Bates
Cover design by Neil Francis

There is a little yellow duck hiding on every page. Can you find it?

This is the Appleby family.

Ollie and Amber are very excited. Today they are going to get their new puppy.

Dad drives them to Hazel Hill's house.

Eight weeks ago, Hazel Hill's dog, Gemma, had six tiny puppies. Ollie gives Gemma a pat.

Ollie and Amber go inside to see the puppies.

They are playing in the kitchen. Gemma looks protectively at her pups. "Which one should we choose?" says Ollie.

"They're all sweet," says Amber.

The smallest puppy runs up to Ollie and Amber. "I like this one best," says Ollie. "Me too," agrees Amber.

They are ready to go home.

Ollie carries the puppy to the car. "She's so little," says Amber, "let's call her Shrimp."

Shrimp meets Felix.

When they get home Ollie shows Shrimp her new bed.
But Shrimp is more interested in Felix, the cat.

They feed Shrimp.

"I think Shrimp's hungry," Ollie says to Amber. "Let's give her something to eat."

Ollie and Amber give Shrimp a bowl of water and some special puppy food. But Shrimp is much too excited to eat.

They take Shrimp outside.

Shrimp isn't allowed to go far until she has her injections.
Ollie and Amber play with her. Felix hides in the tree.

After supper, they put Shrimp to bed.

"Please can I sleep with her?" Amber asks her mother.
"No, you have your own bed, Amber," Mrs. Appleby says.

It's time for bed.

Mr. Appleby carries Amber upstairs. "Come on, sleepyhead," he says. "Goodnight, sleep tight, Shrimp," says Ollie.

The next day, Ollie and Amber get up early.

They want to see their new puppy right away. "Oh no,"
cries Amber. "What a mess!"

There is a big puddle on the floor.

Mrs. Appleby shows it to Shrimp. "Naughty girl," she says softly. Mr. Appleby gets something to clean it up.

Later, the Applebys take Shrimp to the vet.

Shrimp is very excited when she sees all the other animals.
She wants to play with them.

The vet gives Shrimp an injection.

"This won't hurt her!" The vet says. "It's just so that she will not catch any illnesses."

Amber and Ollie put Shrimp on a leash.

They take her out for a walk. "I love our new puppy," says Amber. "Me too," beams Ollie.

This edition published in 2005 by Usborne Publishing Ltd, Usborne House, 83-85 Saffron Hill, London EC1N 8RT, England.
Copyright © 2005, 1992 Usborne Publishing Ltd. www.usborne.com
First published in America in 2005. UE
The name Usborne and the devices ♀ ⊕ are Trade Marks of Usborne Publishing Ltd.